This book belongs to:

....

Note to parents and carers

Read it yourself is a series of classic, traditional tales, written in a simple way to give children a confident and successful start to reading.

Each book is carefully structured to include many high-frequency words that are vital for first reading. The sentences on each page are supported closely by pictures to help with reading, and to offer lively details to talk about.

The books are graded into four levels that progressively introduce wider vocabulary and longer stories as a reader's ability grows.

Ideas for use

- Begin by looking through the book and talking about the pictures. Has your child heard this story before?

- Help your child with any words he does not know, either by helping him to sound them out or supplying them yourself.

- Developing readers can be concentrating so hard on the words that they sometimes don't fully grasp the meaning of what they're reading. Answering the puzzle questions on pages 30 and 31 will help with understanding.

For more information and advice, visit www.ladybird.com/readityourself

Level 1 is ideal for children who have received some initial reading instruction. Each story is told very simply, using a small number of frequently repeated words.

Special features:

stepmother

castle

fairy godmother

first stepsister

second stepsister

shoe

Cinderella

6

7

Careful match between story and pictures

Opening pages introduce key story words

A fairy godmother came to Cinderella's house. She made Cinderella a beautiful dress. She made Cinderella some beautiful shoes.

Large, clear type

14

15

Educational Consultant: Geraldine Taylor

A catalogue record for this book is available from the British Library

Published by Ladybird Books Ltd
80 Strand, London, WC2R ORL
A Penguin Company

2 4 6 8 10 9 7 5 3 1
© LADYBIRD BOOKS LTD MMX
Ladybird, Read It Yourself and the Ladybird Logo are registered or
unregistered trade marks of Ladybird Books Limited.

ISBN: 978-1-40930-351-0

Printed in China

Cinderella

Illustrated by Marina Le Ray

first
stepsister

second
stepsister

6

stepmother

castle

fairy
godmother

shoe

Cinderella

7

Cinderella lived with her stepmother and stepsisters.

Cinderella's stepmother and stepsisters made Cinderella do all the housework.

One day, there was a ball at the castle.

"Can I go to the ball?" asked Cinderella.

"No," said the first stepsister. "You do not have a dress."

"No," said the second stepsister. "You do not have any shoes."

A fairy godmother came to Cinderella's house. She made Cinderella a beautiful dress. She made Cinderella some beautiful shoes.

Cinderella put on her dress.
She put on her shoes.
"Now I can go to the ball,"
she said.

The prince danced with Cinderella. After the ball, the prince found Cinderella's shoe.

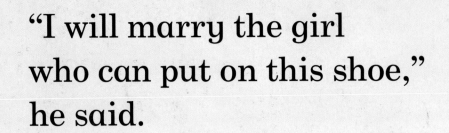

"I will marry the girl
who can put on this shoe,"
he said.

The prince came to
Cinderella's house.

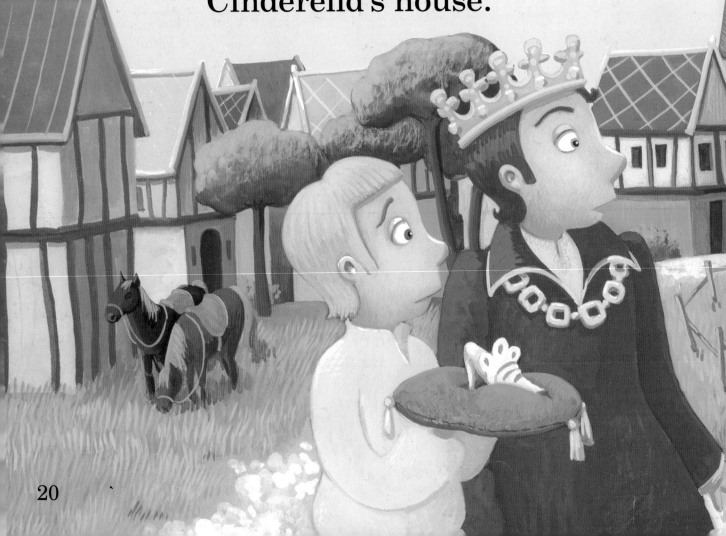

"Is this your shoe?" he asked.

"Yes," said the first stepsister. But the shoe did not fit.

22

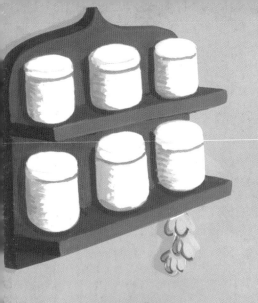

"Is this your shoe?"
asked the prince.
"Yes," said the
second stepsister.
But the shoe did not fit.

"Is this your shoe?"
asked the prince.

"Yes," said Cinderella,
and she put on the shoe.

26

"Will you marry me?"
asked the prince.
"Yes," said Cinderella.
So she did!

How much do you remember about the story of Cinderella? Answer these questions and find out!

- Who did Cinderella live with?

- What did the fairy godmother make for Cinderella to wear?

- How did the prince find Cinderella after the ball?

Look at the pictures from the story and say the order they should go in.

A

B

C

D

Read it yourself
with Ladybird

The Three Billy Goats Gruff

Cinderella

Little Red Hen

Goldilocks and the Three Bears

The Magic Porridge Pot

The Ugly Duckling

The Gingerbread Man

Sleeping Beauty

Sly Fox and Red Hen

The Three Little Pigs

Town Mouse and Country Mouse

Little Red Riding Hood

The Elves and the Shoemaker

Jack and the Beanstalk

The Pied Piper of Hamelin

The Wizard of Oz

Collect all the titles in the series.